The

AMAZING

LIVE

Christmas Tree

Grandma Marcie loved telling stories to her grandchildren and their cousin Zander. Each year at Christmas time she gathered them all together at her house.

She was busy for days before they came, making big spicy cookies, fruity cake and buttery biscuits. When the children finally arrived, all bundled against the cold, the delicious smells of ginger and cinnamon greeted them.

After they had put away their winter coats, scarves and hats and lined up their seventeen pairs of boots all in a row, the children gathered around the big stone fireplace, wrapped in colorful quilts, munching cookies and drinking hot chocolate. Then Grandma would pull her old rocker close and tell their favorite Christmas story. It was their favorite because it was all about them!

PUBLISHER

The

AMAZING
LIVE
Christmas
Tree

MARCELLA BETZLER
Story

DEBORAH MARTIN
Illustrations

Snuggled in a little valley, surrounded by mossy green hills in the summer and bright white snow in the winter, was Grandma Marcie's cottage. Beyond lay the dark, mysterious forest.

It was said that fairies lived there, and tales were told of strange and wonderous things that had happened over the years. Grandma seldom went into the forest any more, but as a child she had played there often. She was always amazed at the many delightful things she found to play with.

One day Grandma looked out her window and saw Smoke, her carrier pigeon, bringing her a letter from the nearby town. Smoke had gotten his name because whether he was coming or going he could disappear very quickly.

The letter he brought was from her grandson. She opened it and read it right away.

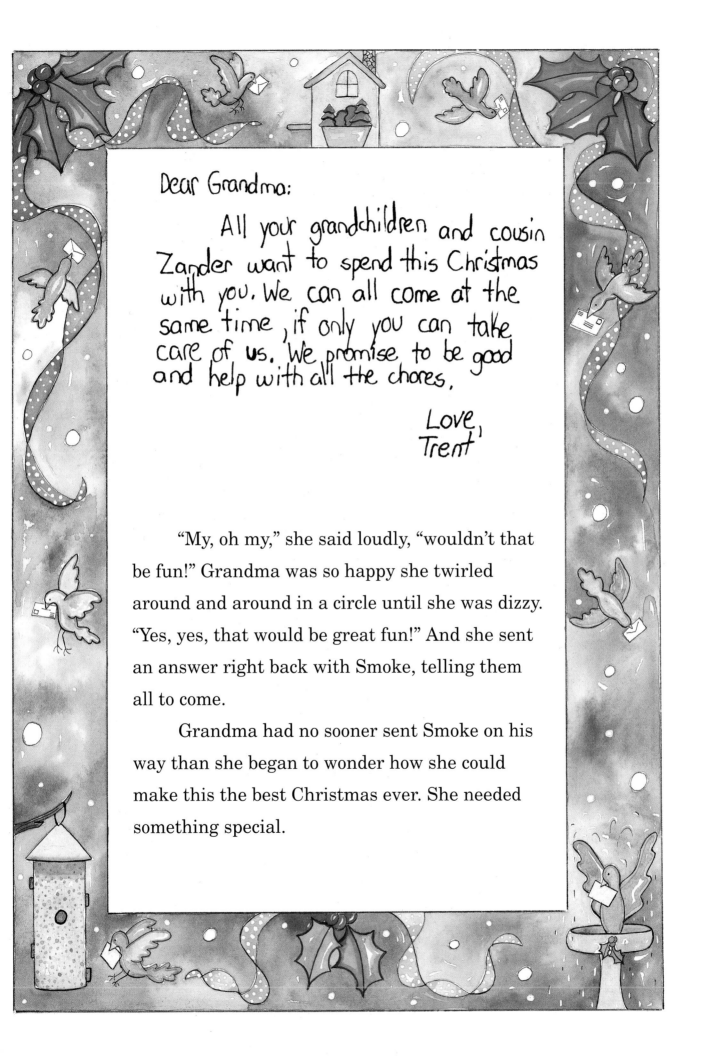

Dear Grandma:

All your grandchildren and cousin Zander want to spend this Christmas with you. We can all come at the same time, if only you can take care of **us**. We promise to be good and help with all the chores.

Love,
Trent

"My, oh my," she said loudly, "wouldn't that be fun!" Grandma was so happy she twirled around and around in a circle until she was dizzy. "Yes, yes, that would be great fun!" And she sent an answer right back with Smoke, telling them all to come.

Grandma had no sooner sent Smoke on his way than she began to wonder how she could make this the best Christmas ever. She needed something special.

Although it was still several weeks before Christmas, Grandma became more and more excited as the days went by.

"I know what I'll do," she said to herself one day, "I'll go pick pine cones in the forest. It will help me think of something to make this Christmas the most special of all."

After a while she grew tired and sat on a log to rest. She put her hands on her head and said, very loudly, "What can I do? Oh, what can I do?"

Suddenly, the log moved, raising Grandma straight up into the air. She quickly leaped to the ground before it got too high. "What in the world was that?" she said, staring at the log. Then she gasped and jumped backward. "That's not a log. It's....it's....an arm! It's a huge arm!"

Grandma closed her eyes for a moment, hoping it would go away. But when she opened them it was still there, and she saw that the arm was connected to a giant and that he appeared to be asleep. Gathering her courage, she carefully tiptoed up to his big ear and yelled, "Wake up! Who are you?" When the giant didn't move, she shouted once more, "Wake up! Who are you?" More quietly, she said, "This looks like the work of the forest fairies to me."

Without moving, the giant rolled his eyes toward Grandma and said softly, "Don't be afraid. I won't harm you."

Grandma quickly stepped back, tripping over a rock in her hurry to get away. The giant, not wanting to frighten her more, whispered, "Please don't go away. I need your help."

Slowly he sat up, repeating, "Please, listen to me!"

"Very well," Grandma replied. "Just don't come any closer!"

Speaking as softly as he could, the giant told Grandma Marcie his story. "Once I was a wood cutter," he began. "One day I was in the forest cutting down a tree, and I saw some delicious-looking red berries. When I stopped to rest, I ate some of them. Soon I fell into a deep sleep. I don't know how long I slept, but when I awoke, I was a giant."

"I knew it!" exclaimed Grandma. "I bet the fairies did this to you! Didn't your mother ever tell you not to eat anything in the forest unless you knew it was safe?" Then, seeing the giant's sad face, she said kindly, "Never mind. I may be able to help you."

Moving a little closer to the giant, she made herself comfortable on a mossy rock. "Many years ago," she began, "my father told me about some magical berries. They grow beside a waterfall, deep in the forest, all year round. If you can find them, they can remove the spell cast by the fairies."

When he heard this good news, the giant shouted with joy. He picked up Grandma Marcie and held her high above the ground.

"You're making me dizzy! Put me down this instant!"

Smiling, the giant placed her back on the ground. "I won't harm you," he said. "Now tell me. How can I repay your kindness?"

Grandma thought for a minute. What on earth could a giant possibly do to help her? Then she remembered the grandchildren and how she wanted to do something special for them for Christmas.

"Well," she said, "maybe you *can* help me. I need something wonderful to surprise my seventeen grandchildren with for Christmas."

Carefully, the giant picked Grandma up and placed her on his shoulder. Then, in a whisper, he said, "What do children like the best about Christmas?"

"That's easy," said Grandma, "Santa Claus. They would love to see him." Then she added, "But that's impossible."

"Maybe not," said the giant. "And what is their second-favorite thing?"

Grandma thought about all the wonderful sights and smells of Christmas, but one thing stood out above all the others.

"The Christmas tree," she said excitedly.

"Right," said the giant. "And that is how I can help you make this Christmas special. I can help them to see Santa Claus in person, and I can find the most incredible Christmas tree ever."

The first thing to do was to find the perfect tree. So with Grandma perched on his shoulder, the giant strode off into the deep forest.

For hours they tramped through the woods, but none of the trees seemed to be just right. They were almost ready to give up for the day when they came upon the most magnificent tree they had ever seen, growing on the very edge of the forest. They stood in silence, gazing at the beautiful tree.

Finally Grandma said, "It's perfect in every way, but it's far too big to move."

But the giant just smiled. "I don't plan to move it. I'm going to build a house around it."

At that, Grandma Marcie danced a little jig on the giant's shoulder. "A live Christmas tree! An *amazing* live Christmas tree! What a wonderful idea!"

"Then," the giant continued, "I'm going to carve seventeen big wooden balls with windows to decorate the tree, one for each child to sleep in."

"Oh heavens!" shouted Grandma. "They *will* be able to see Santa." Still dancing, she added, "And we can paint the balls with bright colors."

With a wide grin, the giant placed Grandma gently on the ground, saying, "Meet me here tomorrow and we will get started."

Grandma walked back to her cottage feeling happier than she had for days, and a catchy little jingle began running through her head. *"Ting a ling, ting a ling, ting a ling a lee,"* she sang.

The following morning the giant showed up with the biggest tool box Grandma had ever seen. For the next few days he worked with such skill and speed that the house quickly took shape. It was very tall, tall enough to completely surround the huge tree, and it had a glass roof that opened to let in air so the tree could breathe. The only things in the big, tall room were a fireplace for Santa Claus to come down and Grandma's rocker.

The days flew by as the giant carved the Christmas-ball beds, and Grandma painted them to look like tree ornaments. She took care to make each one different and printed one name on each ball. When they were all finished she gathered her beautiful hand-made quilts and pillows from home to make up the beds.

At last everything was ready. They had finished just in time. The children would be arriving on the bus in just one day.

Grandma and the giant were happy with all their work, but they were also a little sad. It was time for the giant to leave.

"I'm sorry that you have to go," said Grandma. "It would have been nice if you could stay for Christmas with the children and me."

"I would like that," replied the giant, but I must find the magic berries and return to my own family before Christmas."

Grandma nodded, then she gave him a big hug and they said goodbye.

As she headed home, Grandma Marcie hummed her little tune, *"Ting a ling, ting a ling, ting a ling a lee, Swinging on a live Christmas tree."*

It snowed all that night, and the next morning everything seemed to have a marshmallow topping. The tree branches sparkled, bent low with their heavy burden of newly fallen snow. The only tree spared was the magnificent Christmas tree in the new house.

Soon it was time to meet the children, and Grandma's old, battered, but trustworthy truck went rattling down the hill to the bus depot. When she arrived the children were already getting off the bus, the older ones helping the babies. Lisa was carrying her brother Luke. He had dark hair that stood straight up like a Mohawk cut. Stephanie helped her little sister Allison, a cute brown-eyed girl with chubby legs.

When the children saw Grandma, they all ran toward her at the same time. She was soon overwhelmed by little arms and big kisses. They all piled into the truck and buckled up the special seat belts Grandma had put in for just such an occasion. As cold and drafty as it was, it seemed like heaven to the children as the truck popped, sputtered and rattled in tune with their young voices all the way to Grandma's house.

By the time they got to Grandma Marcie's house, it was snowing hard. This delighted Matthew and Brandon, who jumped off the truck and instantly began to make snowballs to throw at the other children.

Splat! Trent got one in the back of the head. *Zap!* Travis got one too. *Plop!* Zander spun around just in time, but still got two on his back. The three younger boys chased Brandon and Matthew. The fun of the game turned their faces bright red, and their hands became stiff with cold. After several turns around the cottage, they called a truce and went inside to get warm and dry.

The children loved the cottage with its lace curtains and wooden floors. It was cozy and warm, and pleasant smells came from every nook and cranny.

Everyone had brought a sleeping bag and pillow, except for Luke, who had a basket, and Allison, who had a cradle. As they settled down for the night, the little tune kept buzzing in Grandma's head.

"Ting a ling, ting a ling, ting a ling a lee.
Look at you, look at me, peeping out to see,
What we can see, swinging on a live Christmas tree."

In the days that followed, the children played and played. They made snowmen and built a snow house. The two older girls, Nicole and Kimberly, took the two younger ones, Lindsey and Amy, sledding. Karie, Kendyl and Michelle found some old inner tubes and joined them on the hills behind the cottage. They played outside every night until dark, then came staggering inside to the delicious smells of the hot dinner Grandma Marcie had cooked.

After dinner, they might have a rousing pillow fight, and Brett would end the day by telling ghost stories. This would cause some little ones to sleep two in a sleeping bag while keeping one eye open all night.

The day before Christmas came at last. The two babies woke the whole cottage. Luke was wailing for his breakfast, and Allison was flopping over each sleeping bag looking for Stephanie.

Outside, the snow had stopped falling, and long, pointed icicles hung from the eaves. The children slowly wiggled out of their bags and stood at the windows, dreamily imagining rows of upside-down popsicles. This was the day they were going to look for a Christmas tree. At least, that's what Grandma had told them.

Grandma had planned the best way to surprise the children with the tree. She kept them moving quickly, in single file along the path. When the tree house came into view, she gathered the children in a circle around her and told them about the giant and the amazing live Christmas tree. They listened with open mouths, staring in disbelief at the tall, glass-roofed house before them.

Grandma was overjoyed at their reaction and could hardly wait to share what waited for everyone inside.

Zander was the first to reach the house. He turned the big door knob, and Travis and Trent pushed the door open. All the children rushed in and stood in silence at the sight before them.

Grandma finally broke the spell. "Look where you will sleep tonight – each in your own wooden bed! And you won't miss seeing Santa Claus," she said, showing them a whistle around her neck. "I will blow once on my whistle when I hear him coming."

Joining hands, the children and Grandma danced aroung the tree while she sang her little Christmas song.

"Ting a ling, ting a ling, ting a ling a lee.
Look at you, look at me, peeping out to see,
Peeping out to see what we can see,
Swinging on a live Christmas tree.

Singing, swinging, in our wooden beds,
Waiting for Santa and his flying sled.
Bringing lots of toys for you and me,
Swinging on a live Christmas tree.
Ting a ling, ting a ling, ting a ling a lee."

It was getting late, so the children
all climbed into their wooden balls
and settled down for the night. As they
snuggled into their quilts, the balls
swayed gently, soothing them into sleep.

Just as it was becoming impossible to keep their eyes open, the sound of distant sleigh bells was heard. Grandma blew a sharp blast on her whistle and the children bolted upright. They all looked up through the glass roof to the sky beyond, just in time to see the outline of Santa's sleigh crossing the moon. A few seconds later he turned and came back, settling in midair over the tall house.

The children were very quiet. Only their eyes moved as they watched Santa step out of his sleigh onto the chimney. Reaching back, the jolly old fellow pulled out a large sack of toys. Then, with one tremendous swish, he landed in the fireplace with a great thud!

The children had to stop themselves from laughing out loud.

Santa was so much fatter than they had imagined, but his merry *"Ho! Ho! Ho!"* sounded like they thought it would. His beautiful red velvet suit was trimmed with white, and his boots were black and shiny. With a twinkle in his eye, he set the toys beneath the huge tree. He didn't notice the children in the big wooden balls, or if he did, he never let on. Before he left, he stepped back and looked at the tree. Never, in all his travels, had he seen a more amazing Christmas tree.

When Santa was ready to leave, he zoomed up the chimney, laughing merrily. All that could be heard as he flew off into the night was the cracking of his whip and the jingle of his sleigh bells fading into the distance.

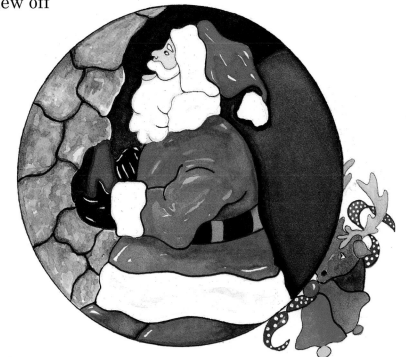

Grandma went outside and saw a trail of stardust float down from the sky. When she returned inside, the children were all fast asleep with big smiles on their glowing faces. It was as if Santa had cast a spell of dreamy happiness over them.

Grandma beamed as she pulled her old shawl snugly around her shoulders. She lit the fireplace and curled up in her rocking chair in front of the fire, knowing she could sleep now. As she closed her eyes, she silently thanked the fairies for sending the giant, who had given her and her grandchildren a most magical Christmas. She thought of the giant, who she knew would not be a giant any more, and wished him and his family the merriest Christmas possible.

Grandma Marcie began to rock in time with the swaying wooden balls.

"Ting a ling, ting a ling, ting a ling a lee.
Ting a ling, ting a ling, ting a ling a lee."

Canadian Cataloging in Publication Data

Betzler, Marcella.
    The amazing live Christmas tree

    ISBN 0-9696097-3-6

    1. Christmas stories. I. Martin, Deborah, 1950–   II. Title.
PZ7.B489Am 1994   J813'.54
C93-091672-7

Production Credits

Executive Producer: Ken Budd
Designer: Ken Budd
Text: Marcella Betzler
Illustrations: Deborah Martin
Music and Words: Marcella Betzler
Music Arranger: Marta Betzler
    Moorehead
Editor: Elaine Jones
Design Assistant: Rory Christianson
Color Separator, Printer & Binder:
    Friesen Printers

Distributor

RAINCOAST BOOKS

Raincoast Books
112 East 3rd Avenue,
Vancouver, B.C. V5T 1C8
Phone: (604) 873 - 6581
Fax: (604) 874 - 2711

Publisher

SummerWild Productions
#2202 1275 Pacific Street,
Vancouver, B.C. V6E 1T6
Phone & Fax: (604) 681 - 0015

Printed in Canada